THE
MIDNIGHT FLIGHT
OF
MOOSE, MOPS AND MARVIN

234567RABP7898765

Library of Congress Cataloging in Publication Data

Bladow, Suzanne.
  The midnight flight of Moose, Mops, and Marvin.

  SUMMARY: Three little mice begin an unusual adven-
ture when they are accidentally caught in one of Santa's
sacks and are left under a Christmas tree.
  [1.   Christmas stories.   2.   Mice—Fiction]
I. Mathieu, Joseph. II. Title.
PZ10.3.B564Mi   [E]   75-8972
ISBN 0-07-005535-1
ISBN 0-07-005536-X lib. bdg.

McGraw-Hill Book Company

New York   St. Louis   San Francisco   Auckland   Düsseldorf   Johannesburg
Kuala Lumpur   London   Mexico   Montreal   New Delhi   Panama
Paris   São Paulo   Singapore   Sydney   Tokyo   Toronto

THE
MIDNIGHT FLIGHT
OF
MOOSE, MOPS AND MARVIN

BY SUZANNE WILSON BLADOW

ILLUSTRATED BY JOSEPH MATHIEU

For Craig and Amy
and for Melanie

In a funny old house in the far North, there lived three mice. They made their home down a crack by a fireplace, in a warm cozy hole under the hearth. There they stayed most of every day, chatting, making up stories and taking little naps.

At night the three mice ventured out. First came the largest mouse, who was called Moose; then Mops, a fuzzy sort of mouse; then Marvin, a jolly mouse with a tail as long as a pumpkin vine.

They had often explored the room above their home. It was a large workroom containing many mysterious objects. There were animals with cotton insides (Mops peeked), and small people-like creatures, some stuffed and some solid and some that would say "Mama" if you bumped them over (Moose did).

Marvin had fun trying out all the mechanical contraptions he found there. He even borrowed some tiny furniture for the mousehold.

Each night they passed through this room, scrunched under a closed door and scampered into the kitchen. There they happily poked into every corner to find tidbits of food.

But the best feast of all came only once a year. Gorgeous smells would beckon them to the kitchen. The person the mice called Keeper of the Kitchen would be dozing in her rocking chair by the fire, all tired out from an unusual amount of baking.

What a yummy feast there would be for Moose, Mops and Marvin! Plump raisins and candied fruit scattered in a dusting of flour, sweet nuts in a wooden bowl, crunchy bread crumbs mixed with strange-tasting herbs, and bits of pie crust dough.

One night, the mice recognized the sounds that always came before the great feast: voices talking excitedly, doors slamming and footsteps pattering quickly across the workroom floor.

Moose remarked, "Isn't it rather warm for this late at night?" Indeed, the fire was still lit in the fireplace above them.

Mops started hopping up and down. "It's late, fellows, and they're still up there bustling around."

"This is the night!" said Marvin. "I can hardly wait until everyone leaves."

The three gazed anxiously up their passageway, almost overcome
by the faint mouth-watering smells coming from the distant kitchen.

At last all was quiet. But to be certain, they waited for the final
signal, which they knew so well. A signal which, for some reason,
always began as a jouncing, jingling sound of harness bells and then
faded away.

"There it is," squeaked Marvin. The jingling stopped. "Let's go!"

And they raced up the passageway, tore out of the mousehole at top speed—and tumbled over a big lumpy sack in the middle of the floor.

They picked themselves up and sat on their haunches to study the situation.

"What's this big lumpy sack doing here?" chattered Mops nervously. "It's never been here before. Maybe we ought to go back."

"I don't know, Mops," said Moose. "But maybe we ought to hurry on." He glanced longingly toward the kitchen. "Let's not worry about it now."

"Oh me," said Marvin. "I really don't know what…" He stopped, tilting his head and listening.

"What's wrong, Marvin?" asked Mops.

"Don't you hear the bells? They're coming back!" whispered Marvin.

Outside, footsteps crunched in the snow.

The mice stared at one another. Then all three realized they were too far from both the mousehole and the kitchen to escape.

"Into the sack, boys!" cried Marvin. And zip! Zip! Zip! It was done.

The door banged open and a voice boomed out, "Well, there it is. I thought I was short one sack of toys when I took off."

Crowded by strangely shaped objects in the sack's dark insides, the shivering mice felt themselves swinging upward and over and landing with a thump. Footsteps crunching, cold outdoor air blowing through the sack, another thump! Then—jingling, jouncing.

The three frightened creatures huddled paw in paw, with quivering tails wrapped around one another.

"You know, fellows," said Moose, "I believe we're going on a trip."

"The only way to find out," declared Marvin, "is to look." And he bravely chewed a peephole in the rough cloth sack. "Hmph. Not the snack I expected tonight," he said around a mouthful. "A sack is not a snack."

He squinted one eye and put the other to the hole. "My word. My word!"

"What?" cried the others.

"Well, friends, we're up!" He turned to them and whispered, "I mean, we're flying."

Moose and Mops jostled each other to get to the tiny window in the sack. Moose won out, looked and turned back to Marvin in astonishment while Mops had his turn. Then they all sat back and looked at one another in the faint starlight.

"Well," said Moose. "What to do?"

"We could get out of the sack," said Mops brightly. Then he added sadly, "but that's all."

"I vote we stay inside," said Marvin. Before he could go on, their flight ceased. The three crowded to the hole.

"Let me see too!" begged Mops.

"Make your own places," grumbled Marvin. They quickly did.

"Someone's climbing into a chimney with a sack," said Moose.

"Now he's coming back," warned Mops.

"Whee! We're in a sleigh that flies. How about that!" said Marvin in a hushed sort of squeal.

"Look at the funny animals pulling us," said Mops.

"I've seen that man in the workroom," Moose exclaimed.

"You know what's in this sack with us?" asked Marvin. "I can see now. Things from the workroom. What did he call them? Oh, yes. Toys."

The sleigh flew and landed again and again. The little mice grew tired of looking out, so they curled up, nestling among some soft and furry stuffed animals.

"Are we toys too?" wondered Mops sleepily.

No one answered. Moose and Marvin were already asleep.

They awoke, startled. Their sack was being lifted up and thrown over the man's shoulder. They whizzed downward with him. His big hand reached in and took out some of the toys, and they shot upward with him. Many times they did this. Down the chimneys, up the chimneys. At last there were only a few toys left with them.

"Hey, fellows," Moose worried, "what'll we do? He's going to find us next time."

"We must hide," urged Marvin. "And quickly."

He disappeared into a doll's apron pocket. Mops slipped the catch on a jack-in-the-box, climbed inside and managed to pull Jack back in with him as he closed the lid. Poor Moose thought he'd never find a place, but a stuffed kangaroo baby had room for him in its mother's pouch.

Sure enough, they were taken out of the sack after the very next downward trip. The man gave a happy sigh, and all became quiet.

They had been left behind. One by one, the mice peeked out of their hiding places. What a sight!

Never had they seen such lights, such brightly colored lights, all fastened on the branches of a pine tree directly above them. Around them were stacks of boxes wrapped with shimmering paper and ribbon.

"Where are we?" asked Moose.

"I don't know," said Mops. "But whee!" And he skittered up the tree.

The other two joined in the game, playing tag and hide-and-seek among the shiny ornaments. From the top, clinging and swaying under a golden angel, Marvin spied something else.

"Look over there," he squeaked, pointing to the fireplace.

The three raced across the room and up to the mantel where bulgy stockings hung.

"One for each!" shrilled Mops.

And they dived in.

Lovely sweets. Candy, hard and sugary, soft and gooey. Walnuts that yielded to knowing mouse teeth. Here was their feast at last.

Hardly had they taken two bites, when Moose interrupted. "Shhh. Listen."

The three poked their heads out. Up above them, someone was waking up. There were squeals of "Christmas is here!"

The mice moved fast, down to the floor in close formation and around the room. Where to hide? Marvin spied a crack and in they went, just in time to avoid a stampede of bare and slippered feet.

What noise! Happy yelps and "Thank you's."

"Mama, what's this?" said a little girl's voice.

"Oh, John," said a woman, "could a mouse have been in the stockings? Look at this candy."

"Sure looks like it," said a man. "We'd better let Tasha up from the basement."

Peering out cautiously, Moose, Mops and Marvin jumped back in a hurry when they saw a tan, furry animal leap into the room.

The most frightening part of their journey had begun.

"Mouse, Tasha," said the smaller boy. "Find the mouse."

From their shallow hole the mice watched the cat, who went sniffing from the tree to the sticky stockings.

All day Tasha roamed the room. But part of the time was spent pouncing on pieces of wrapping paper and ribbon and batting the baubles that hung from the tree.

That evening, as the family turned off the lights and went up-stairs, the bigger boy said to the cat, "We're leaving you in charge, Tasha. Try to remember what a mouse looks like."

The cat began to prowl seriously, coming closer and closer to the hiding place. Quite near it, she stopped short and sniffed around thoroughly. The mice clung together, all trembly. But something caused Tasha to hesitate. A mousey sound from the dining room? She dashed away.

After a while, Moose asked in a mouse whisper, "Do you suppose she's given up?"

"Just a minute, I'll go see," said Mops helpfully.

Marvin put a firm paw on Mops' tail, just in time.

Two glowing eyes stared in at them!

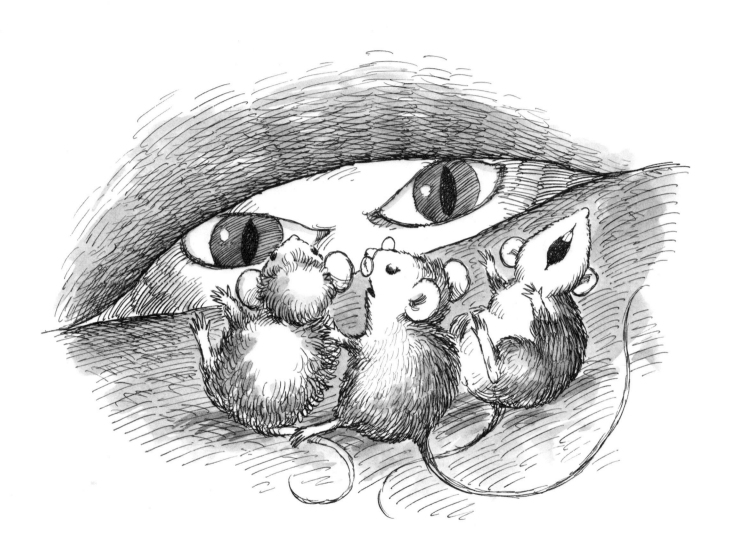

Suddenly there was a jingling of harness bells, and scuffling sounds came from the cold fireplace. The cat's ears twitched. Then she was gone.

The mice stared at the fireplace. There was that familiar whiz, and the workroom man landed on both booted feet and stepped out. He peered around in the dimness, inspecting a crack in one corner and a loose baseboard.

"Mice?" he called softly. "This is Santa. Please come out. Mrs. Santa's been so worried about you—she wasn't really asleep when you came to the kitchen every Christmas Eve, you see."

He sighed and sat down on the floor, muttering to himself. "I thought I was pretty smart, figuring they hid in that last sack. But I've been back to all the houses where I took it. This is the last. If they're not here…" He gave a great yawn. "I can wait a little while."

He took a handful of crumbs from his pocket.

"Mice? Listen, I can't go back without you. Mrs. Santa wants you back, because she loves you, you know…"

His voice trailed off, and his head nodded forward. The mice heard the steady snores of a person who has been awake two nights in a row.

"Does he mean those goodies for us?" asked Moose.

"It's hard to say," hissed Marvin. "But whatever happens, it's better than being caught by that Tasha."

Bravely, Marvin led the way out of the hole. The others followed, each holding on to the tail in front of him.

"Anyway," whispered Moose trustingly, "I believe in that Santa. I believe he's going to take us home."

They took the crumbs so carefully, Santa didn't even feel their usually ticklesome paws. Looking for more, they each climbed up and into a pocket of his warm red coat, ate a filling snack and snuggled down in contented slumber.

The little mice were very tired after the excitement of their adventurous journey and the terror of Tasha. They slept soundly until Santa's voice woke them.

"Should I say, 'Darling, I have some bad news?' No. 'Dear, I didn't find them, but I'll go back...'"

Unseen by Santa, each mouse poked a nose out. There was a cold, biting wind. "Where are we?" Mops whispered. Then he saw they were back on the doorstep of the old house. They were home!

The door swung open, and there was the Keeper of the Kitchen.

"I thought I heard you." Her face lit up with a beautiful smile. "You found them!"

"No, dear," Santa began.

"But what is this? And this? And this?" She gently touched the three pockets where bright eyes blinked and whiskers twitched busily at the welcoming sights and smells of home.

"What do you know!" exclaimed Santa boomingly, and Moose, Mops and Marvin popped out of sight.

"Oh come, dear creatures! See what I have for you!" coaxed Mrs. Santa.

Moose peeked out to see, but Marvin chose that moment to scramble from pocket to pocket and round up the others. They jumped to the floor and ran for home. Home! But at the brink of the mousehole all three stood on their haunches, fascinated. On the hearth was a small tree, glittering with tiny ornaments.

"And here's your feast! Merry Christmas!"

Hearing Mrs. Santa's voice so near, they took off, skidding down the passageway. Nuts and breadcubes, crumbs and raisins rained about them. They settled down to sort it out.

"Are we dear creatures?" asked Moose, with his mouth full.

"I'll bet we are," said Mops, tossing raisins in a corner. "I'm fairly sure now we aren't toys."

"Ah, fellows," chuckled Marvin, neatly stacking breadcubes. "With what we've learned—"

"I learned to watch out for Tashas," Mops interrupted.

Marvin went on. "The stories we can tell!"

Then they all had a snack. The only sound in the mousehole was of munching, as each of them began planning the way he would tell the story of how they had flown through the starry winter night.